Macmillan Publishing Company
866 Third Avenue, New York, N.Y. 10022
Collier Macmillan Canada, Inc.
Produced for the publishers by
Sadie Fields Productions Ltd, London
Printed in Italy.
First American edition 1985

10 9 8 7 6 5 4 3 2 1

Library of Congress Cataloging in Publication Data

Krauze, Andrzej, date.
Reggie rabbit plants a garden.
Summary: When spring comes, a rabbit takes every step
to beautify his garden by planting, pruning, clipping,
and mowing.
1. Children's stories, American. [1. Rabbits –
Fiction. 2. Gardening – Fiction] I. Title.
PZ7.K8757Re 1985   [E]   84-12615
ISBN 0-02-750960-5

REGGIE RABBIT PLANTS A GARDEN

Andrzej Krauze

Macmillan Publishing Company
New York

Hum de hum. I can't wait for Spring!

Oh my, it's getting warmer.

I can even see some little buds.

It's time to get out my ladder . . .

and start pruning my trees.

Get rid of all the dead leaves.

Dump them into a pile.

Plant a nice young tree.

Now I'm ready to dig.

Make some lovely furrows.

Plant the seeds in neat rows.

Give them a little water.

Mow the grass.

Put some plants into the bed.

Just look how my garden is growing!